THESEUS and the MINOTAUR

RETOLD AND ILLUSTRATED BY
WARWICK HUTTON

Margaret K. McElderry Books
NEW YORK

Other books by Warwick Hutton

BEAUTY AND THE BEAST
ADAM AND EVE
JONAH AND THE GREAT FISH
NOAH AND THE GREAT FLOOD
MOSES IN THE BULRUSHES
THE NOSE TREE
THE TINDERBOX

Copyright © 1989 by Warwick Hutton .

Margaret K. McElderry Books
Macmillan Publishing Company
866 Third Avenue
New York, NY 10022
Collier Macmillan Canada, Inc.

Printed in Singapore

10 9 8 7 6 5 4 3 2

Library of Congress Cataloging-in-Publication Data

Hutton, Warwick.
Theseus and the Minotaur/Warwick Hutton.—1st ed.
p.   cm.
Summary: Recounts how Theseus killed the monster, Minotaur, with
the help of Ariadne.
ISBN 0-689-50473-X
1. Theseus (Greek mythology)—Juvenile literature. 2. Minotaur
(Greek mythology)—Juvenile literature. [1. Theseus (Greek
mythology) 2. Minotaur (Greek mythology) 3. Mythology, Greek.]
I. Title.
BL820.T5H87 1989   398.2′1′0938—dc19   88-26875   CIP   AC

Every nine years, the people of Athens had to make a
dreadful payment in tribute to Minos, king of Crete,
because one of his sons had been killed in Athens. He
swore that if they failed to do so, he would destroy their
city. So seven young men and seven girls were sent to
Minos for his monster son—half man, half bull—the
Minotaur. What became of them no one ever knew. But
always they disappeared into the Cretan Labyrinth, where
the monster lived, and were never seen again.

Theseus was the son of Aegeus, king of Athens. He was
young and brave, and had newly arrived at his father's
court. When he heard the sound of distant wailing and
learned of the tribute, he made his way straight down to
the harbor.

There, in the sunlight, by a black-sailed ship, he could see
the doomed young men and girls, with their parents
weeping beside them.

"Wait," Theseus called out. "I will go to Crete, and I will try to kill the Minotaur. If I succeed no one will ever have to go again," said Theseus. "And if we all return alive it will be with a white sail, not this mournful black one. So if you watch from a distance when the boat returns, you'll be able to tell if we're safe." His father, Aegeus, wept to see Theseus go, but he agreed to the plan. A white sail was loaded onto the ship, and one happy young man was left behind in place of Theseus. The north wind blew gently as they set out.

The cruel King Minos came down the hill, with his daughter, Ariadne, at his side, to see his new tribute arriving in Crete. "My payment for the Minotaur!" he cried. "I will keep one of the girls for myself this time." Theseus watched with fury in his throat as Minos chose one girl.

"By Poseidon, God of the Sea, if you touch her I'll kill you!" he said. Minos laughed a deep, long laugh and, pulling off one of his golden rings, hurled it out into the blue sea. "If Poseidon is your god, he'll help you to find my ring. Only if you do will I leave this girl alone."

Without hesitating, Theseus dived into the waves. He swam down so deep that when he opened his eyes it was dark. From the darkness a small light gleamed. Whether it was with Poseidon's help or just by chance he never knew, but there was the ring. On the shore again, dripping and victorious, he returned it to Minos. Ariadne looked long and admiringly at Theseus.

When the doomed young people were marched up from the shore, Ariadne left her father's side to walk with Theseus. She began to talk. She told him how she hated her half brother, the Minotaur, and of the dark and terrible labyrinth in which he lived. It was a huge maze of corridors, chambers, and stairways, from which no one could ever find his way out. After a while, she stopped and whispered: "If you will take me away from here and marry me, I will show you how to kill the monster and save all your companions as well."

Theseus looked around at his young friends and then back to the ship in the harbor. "I will take you away, Ariadne, if you will show me how to kill the Minotaur and find a way through the Labyrinth."

"Be ready this night and I will come to you," she answered.

Late that evening she came and, with her own palace key, slipped Theseus out of his prison room. She took him from the palace and down to a small doorway in the wall of the great building. There she stopped and brought out three objects. "Here is a torch to light the way, a sword to kill the Minotaur, and a ball of wool with a weight in it. When I was a small child, the palace builder, Daedelus, showed me how to use it. Tie the loose end of the wool to the door lintel. Then the ball will roll slowly down the sloping floors of the Labyrinth passages and stairways until

it reaches the center, which is the lowest point. There you will find the monster, who should be sleeping by now. You must kill him. After that, follow the wool back here to me, and we can escape."

Theseus tied the wool to the door, dropped the ball to the passage floor, and entered the darkness of the Labyrinth. The rolling ball led him gently downward toward the center of the maze. The air grew thicker and warmer, and soon a bitter animal smell stung his nose. At length he entered a vast chamber.

Bones were scattered around, and on a large gold bed,
half covered in straw, the Minotaur lay snoring in his sleep.

As Theseus stepped carefully over to the bed, the monster awoke. He bellowed with rage and staggered upright to crush Theseus with his great hands. Despite the thick stench and deep, wild roars, Theseus bravely cut and struck with the sword until the monster half-man lay dead.

Theseus was bruised, cut, and weary, but slowly and carefully he followed the woolen thread upward until he reached Ariadne and the cool night air at the entrance.

Sitting in a field of wildflowers, he told her how he had killed the Minotaur. When he had finished she said, "Quickly, we must free the others and escape before my half brother's death is discovered."

With her keys Ariadne let out the seven young girls and the six young men, and quietly they ran down the seashore road to their ship. In the darkness they pushed off and hoisted the sail.

As dawn spread across the sky, they sailed northward
toward home, away from Minos and his murdered son.

After two days' sailing, they reached the island of Naxos.
Theseus anchored the ship in a quiet bay. The young
people ran up the beach to gather food and get fresh water.
By afternoon, everyone had returned except Ariadne.
"She's sleeping in the shade," said one of the girls.

Theseus was silent at first. Then he looked across the bay
and said, "She is the daughter of Minos. It would not be
safe to take her back with us now. Pull up the anchor; we

must leave her here. I will return for her when the people
of Athens know how she has helped me and what has
happened." The others looked at him in surprise, but they
agreed. Theseus headed the ship out to sea, leaving
Ariadne asleep on Naxos.

Evening came as Theseus sailed away to the north.
Ariadne woke and found Theseus had left her. Alone on the
shore, she wept.

Before long, as the sun began to set over the sea, a strange procession appeared on Naxos. At the head was Dionysus, the God of Feasting. Then came his followers, the horse-tailed satyrs, and girls who were dancing. Soon all were singing and dancing in the evening light. Dionysus found Ariadne, comforted her gently, and took her to join the revels. By the next morning he had persuaded her to forget Theseus and marry him instead.

Theseus, far out to sea, sailed on. He did not speak to the others. He was thinking of the springs and wildflowers of Crete, and of Minos and the Minotaur, and of Ariadne, who had saved them all. For this he had promised to marry her, and now, though he intended to return, he had deserted her on Naxos. Would the gods notice what he had done? Would they understand why? As the ship drew near to Athens something tugged at his memory.

There was great joy and happiness among his companions when they landed on their own shore, but Theseus knew from the way people looked at him that something was wrong. "You said if you were safe you would hoist the white sail! Did you forget?" the people asked. "Your father, King Aegeus, watched and watched from the clifftop for your ship to come back. When at last he saw it far out in the distance with its black sail still up, he thought you must be dead. He stumbled, weeping, to his feet, and then fell from the cliff to the sea below. Theseus, your father is dead. You are now our king."

Then Theseus was overcome with sorrow. He had been thinking only of Ariadne and Crete. Gently, the people led him to his home to grieve. In the following weeks, he had a huge monument built to honor his father. Only then was Theseus crowned the new king of Athens.

And so that the name of Aegeus would never be
forgotten, the blue water around Athens was named the
Aegean Sea. It is still called that today.